Goodbye, Charlie.

In loving memory of my dad

First published in Great Britain in 2021 by Andersen Press Ltd.,
20 Vauxhall Bridge Road, London SW1V 2SA
Originally published in the USA by Feiwel and Friends,
an imprint of Macmillan, 175 5th Ave, New York, NY 10010
Copyright © 2021 by Matthew Cordell.

Printed and bound in China.

1 3 5 7 9 10 8 6 4 2

British Library Cataloguing in Publication Data available.
ISBN 978 1 83913 118 9

BEAR ISLAND

Matthew Cordell

ANDERSEN PRESS

On a lake, there was a house.

There was Louise, Mum and Dad.

There was... Charlie.

On that lake, there was an island.

After breakfast, Louise put on her boots and cap.

"I'm going out on the boat," she said.

Louise thought about Charlie. How he loved the water. How he loved the breeze on his face. How he loved to explore the island.

Louise tied up the boat.
It was quiet on the island.
She looked around.

After a long time alone, she picked up a stick and thwacked a tree.

"I'm leaving!" she announced.

When suddenly, all around, there were butterflies...

Circling, flying, flitting about.

A chipmunk came to investigate.

A couple of deer sprang from the bush and approached carefully and curiously.

Something new and good was happening on the island. Something new and good was happening in Louise.

CRACK! CHUFF!

But then... came a noise.

A crunching of leaves noise...

A snapping of trees noise...

A chuffing of breath noise...

Louise staggered back, afraid.

Afraid yet... angry.

Angry to be *made* afraid.
Angry about Charlie.

Angry about here, now,
and before.

RO

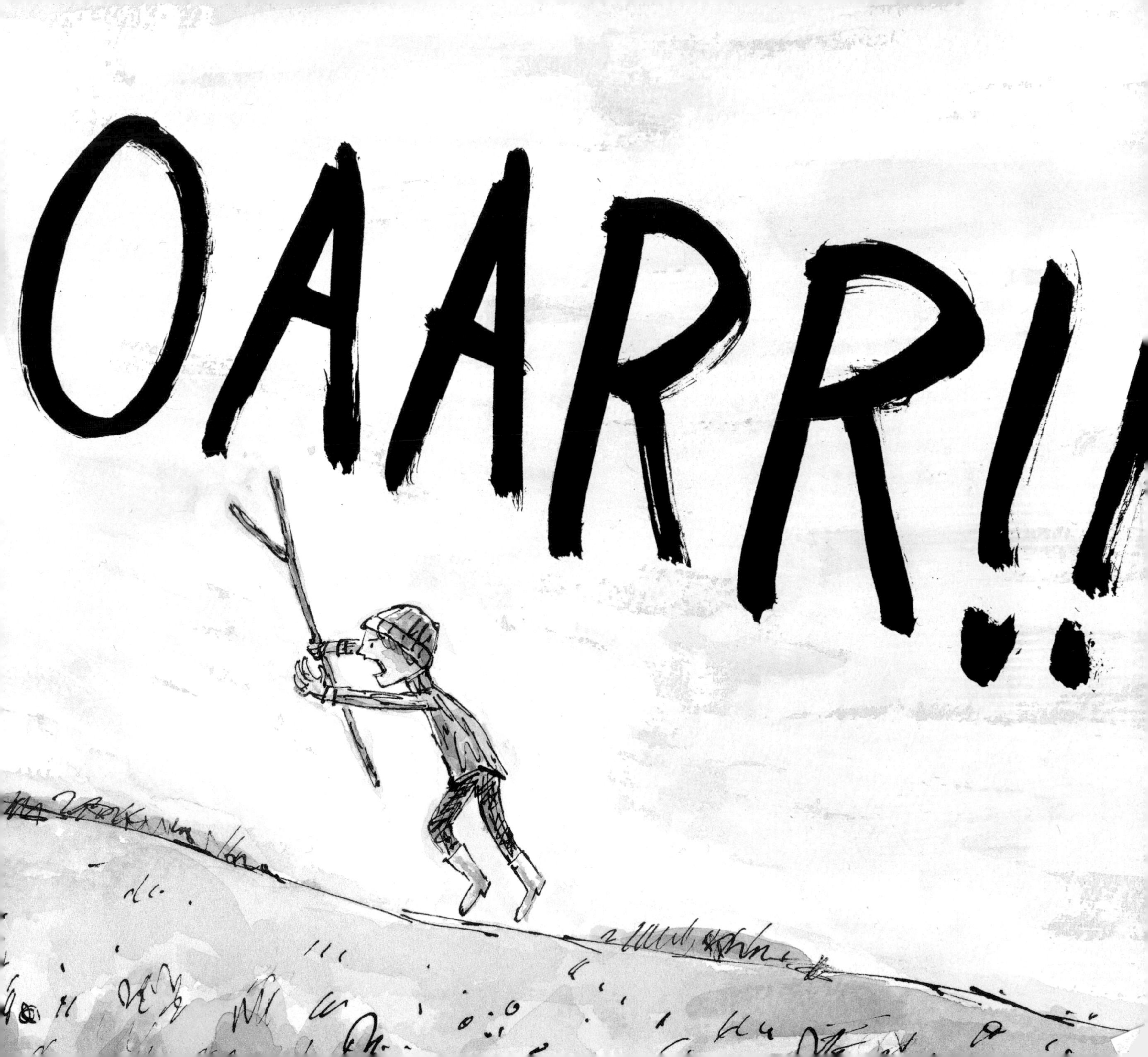
OAARR!!

The bear sank down to the ground. Louise crept back to the boat.

Before going away, she looked again.

This bear.

A familiar feeling. A familiar sadness.

The next day and the days after that, Louise returned to the island.

Some days, only Louise was better.

Some days, only Bear was better.

Then some days, and more and more days, both Louise and Bear became better.

Together.

They were changing on the island.

And they were changing at home.

Winter was coming. The days were getting shorter.
But Louise continued to visit the island.

Until one morning, Bear was not there. She searched everywhere.

At last she found him.

Preparing his den.

Ready to bed down for winter.

"Don't go!" Louise begged.

But it was time for Bear to sleep.

Goodbye, Bear.

"It's not fair...," thought Louise.

"…when the things we love must end."

Rest in Peace
CHARLIE

But sometimes the end…

...is also a beginning.

On the first warm day of spring, Louise and Milly took the boat to the island. Milly did not love the water. She did not love the wind in her face. But she did love to explore.

They searched everywhere for Bear... but he wasn't there.

Had he ever been?

Louise thought for a while.

Then she rowed the
boat back home.

And she smiled.